When MOGGIE and FROGGIE met DOGGIE

By
Julia Stebbing

Illustrated by
Stephen Stone

Sticky Bun
PUBLISHING

This tale is all about a Moggie

Who, one day, encountered Doggie

While out seeking mice to eat.

How he enjoyed a tea-time treat!

As he slowly walked around
He heard an unfamiliar sound
Coming from a place up high -
A yelping, whimpering, whining cry.

Looking up, what did he see?

A creature clinging to a tree,

Quite long and furry, black and white.

Poor Moggie! He had such a fright

"You look so funny hanging there."
Moggie could not help but stare.

The high-pitched whining cry persisted.
"Come down now!" young Mog insisted.

"**D**o not talk to me like that,
You interfering pussy cat!"

Growled Dog, his anger showing clearly.
"I do not want you coming near me."

"You look such a silly Doggie,"
Boldly stated fearless Moggie.

Suddenly, in one big bound,
Doggie leapt without a sound,

And with a most enormous splat
He landed on the ground, quite flat.

Dog shook his fur and licked his paws
And then inspected all his claws.
"I have a perfect explanation
For this awkward situation.

When I was walking near this tree
A strange frog started chasing me.

What could I do? I had to hide.
Frankly, I was terrified."

"Was he very emerald green,
The strangest frog you've ever seen?"
"Yes, indeed," retorted Doggie.
"I know who it is!" cried Moggie.

The day that Froggie and I met,

A day I'll surely not forget,

He was not at all polite

And, like you, I caught a fright.

But as we chatted, I could tell

We would get on really well.

Guess what? I am on my way
To meet him – will you come and play?"

Doggie sniffed and looked unsure -
He'd never had a friend before.
"Come on, Doggie, come with me.
You'll like Froggie, wait and see."

Straight away began a race
And Doggie moved at quite a pace,

But Moggie swiftly followed after.
Listen. Can you hear their laughter?

They ran towards a wooden log
On which serenely sat a Frog,
Looking calm and rather smug –
He'd just enjoyed a juicy slug.

"Hallo buddies," Froggie croaked,

Then smiled at Doggie as he joked,

"I see you've met my good friend Moggie.

My, you are a lucky Doggie.

I'm sorry if I frightened you,
(It wasn't difficult to do!)

And when you ran away to hide
I laughed so much I nearly cried.
Let's play a game of hide and seek.
You two run off and I won't peek."

Moggie said, "Dog, hide with me
While Froggie counts to twenty-three
And when he looks up, we'll be gone.
Come on Doggie, quick, come on!"

Froggie counted, eyes shut tight

And got to twenty-three all right.

Gazing round he heard the sound

Of leaves a 'scrunching on the ground.

Then hip hip hopping, with a croak,
He made his way towards an oak.

They weren't there. Where could they be?
Surely near another tree?

But when he searched, and search he did,
He still could not find where they'd hid.

By now Froggie felt downhearted,
Almost wishing he'd not started.
Looking round he spied a rock
And then, to his enormous shock,
Two tails stuck out on either side.
He felt so glad, he almost cried.

"I have found you, there you are!
I'm pleased you didn't go too far,"
And over to his friends he hurried,
Pretending he had not been worried.

"You know that I'm good friends with Moggie,"
Froggie said and turned to Doggie.

"Perhaps I can be friends with you.
Is that something that you'd like too?"

Said Doggie, "Nothing I'd like more,"
And smiling he stretched out his paw.

And that's how Moggie, also Froggie,
One day became good friends with Doggie.

The End.

We would love you to join the **Sticky Bun Readers Club.**
https://www.stickybunpublishing.com/freedownload

Members of the club get a free download
and we will email you every now and then
and let you know when a new book is coming out.
There's no catch and we will keep emails to a minimum.

And of course, if ever you want to leave the Readers Club
all you need do is unsubscribe.

Authors love reviews so if you can leave one on Amazon
that would be great!

First published in 2021 by
Sticky Bun Publishing

Text © Julia Stebbing
Illustration/Book Design © Stephen Stone

A CIP catalogue record for this book is
available from the British Library.

ISBN 978-1-8382652-3-6

Printed in Great Britain
by Amazon